For David, Nanette,
Sarah and Rowan – H. L.
For my dear friend Sara – A. B.

Barefoot Books
2067 Massachusetts Ave
Cambridge, MA 02140

Text copyright © 1999 and 2010 by Hugh Lupton
Illustrations copyright © 2010 by Agnese Baruzzi
The moral rights of Hugh Lupton and Agnese Baruzzi have been asserted
First published in the United States of America in 2010 by Barefoot Books Inc.
All rights reserved

This book was printed in China by Printplus Ltd on 100% acid-free paper
Reproduction by Grafiscan, Verona

This book was typeset in Captain Kidd Demo, Calligraph421
and Mary Jane. The illustrations were prepared as digital collage

ISBN 978-1-84686-258-8

Library of Congress Cataloging-in-Publication Data is
available under LCCN 2008028156

1 3 5 7 9 8 6 4 2

Tales of
MYSTERY
and MAGIC

Retold by HUGH LUPTON

Illustrated by AGNESE BARUZZI

Barefoot Books
Celebrating Art and Story

Contents

The Blackbird
and his Wife
INDIAN

Once upon a time there lived a blackbird and his wife and they sang so sweetly together that everyone who passed beneath the tree where they lived would stop and listen. It was the most beautiful music you could ever hear; it was as though gold and silver rain was falling into your ears.

One day the king was passing under the tree and he heard the two birds singing.

He said to his servants, "Catch those birds! I will keep them in a silver cage above my bed and they will sing me to sleep at night and they will sing me awake in the morning!"

So the servants set a trap, but they only caught one of the birds; they caught the blackbird's wife. They put her into a silver cage and hung her over the king's bed. But she was so sad that she wouldn't sing at all.

As for the blackbird, when he saw that his wife had been trapped, he was very angry. He took a sharp thorn for a sword and tied it to his waist. He took half a walnut shell and wore it on his head as a helmet. With the other half, he made himself a drum.

Soon he was marching toward the king's palace, beating the drum:
RAT-TAT-TAT, RAT-TAT-TAT!
On the way he met a fox.
"Where are you going, Mr. Blackbird?"
"I'm on my way to fight the king!"
"I'll come with you. For years he's hounded me and hunted me."
"Then jump into my ear," said the blackbird.

RAT-TAT-TAT, RAT-TAT-TAT!
Next the blackbird met a rope.
"Where are you going, Mr. Blackbird?"
"I'm on my way to fight the king!"
"I'll come with you. For years he's tied me and tangled me."
"Then jump into my ear."

RAT-TAT-TAT, RAT-TAT-TAT!
Next the blackbird met some ants.
"Where are you going, Mr. Blackbird?"
"I'm on my way to fight the king!"
"We'll come with you. For years he's poisoned us and poured hot water into our nests."
"Then jump into my ear."

6

RAT-TAT-TAT, RAT-TAT-TAT!

Next the blackbird met a river.

   "Where are you going, Mr. Blackbird?"

   "I'm on my way to fight the king."

   "I'll come with you. For years he's drained me and dirtied me."

   "Then jump into my ear."

So the river jumped into the blackbird's ear and found a place beside the others. And the blackbird marched along until he came to the king's palace. RAT-TAT-TAT, RAT-TAT-TAT! He marched up the golden steps to the palace door, and he knocked: THUMP, THUMP, THUMP.

A servant came and opened the door.

The blackbird drew his sword from his belt and said, "I've come to fight the king!"

And the servant smiled behind his hand at the blackbird, but he led him to where the king was sitting on his golden throne.

"What do you want?" said the king.

"I want my wife," said the blackbird.

"Well, you can't have her!"

"Then," said the blackbird, "we're at war, you and I."

And he began to beat his drum: RAT-TAT-TAT, RAT-TAT-TAT!

The king laughed, then he said
to his servants, "Take this insolent
bird to the henhouse and throw
him in with the chickens —
they'll have pecked him to pieces
by morning."

So the blackbird was taken
and locked inside the
henhouse.

9

Straight away he called to the fox, who came
creeping out of his ear and snarled and snapped at the
chickens — and the chickens were terrified. All night they
huddled in the corner of the coop, quivering and quaking,
and they wouldn't go near the blackbird. And the next
morning, when the servants opened the doors, there was the blackbird, as
right as rain, marching backward and forward, beating his little drum: RAT-
TAT-TAT, RAT-TAT-TAT!

When the king heard that the blackbird was still alive he was angry.

"Tonight," the king said, "take him to the stable and throw him in with
the wild horses — they'll have kicked him to bits by morning."

So that night the blackbird was locked in the stable. Straight away he called to the rope, which came winding out of his ear, lashing and cracking like a whip — and the horses were terrified.

All night they lay in their stalls, quivering and quaking, and they wouldn't go near the blackbird. The next morning, when the servants opened the doors, there was the blackbird, as right as rain, marching backward and forward and beating his little drum: RAT-TAT-TAT, RAT-TAT-TAT!

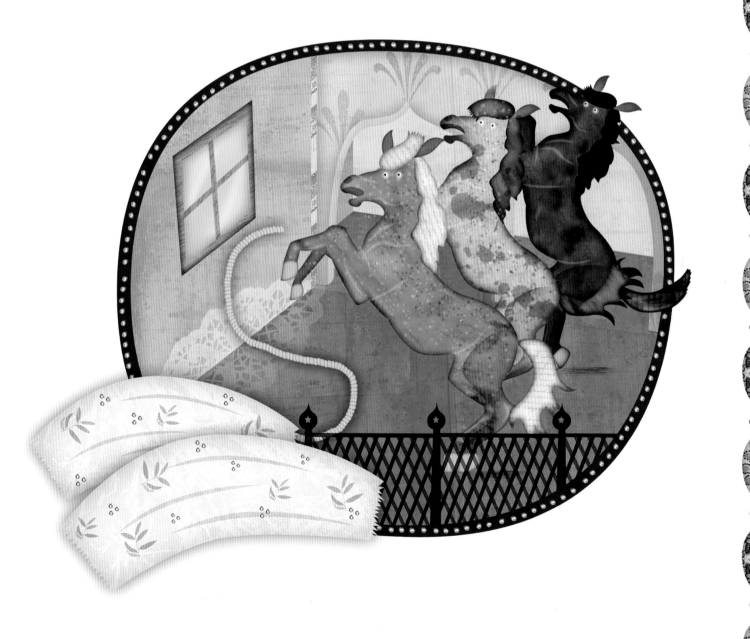

This time the king was furious. "Tonight," he shouted, "take him to the compound and throw him in with the elephants — they'll have trampled him to a pulp by morning."

So that night the blackbird was locked in the elephant compound. Straight away he called to the ants, and the ants came teeming out of his ear. Soon they were crawling up the elephants' trunks and into their ears, tickling and stinging until the elephants lay on the ground, quivering and quaking and begging to be left alone. And the next morning, when the servants opened the doors, there was the blackbird, as right as rain, beating his little drum: RAT-TAT-TAT, RAT-TAT-TAT!

And this time the king was beside himself with rage. "Tonight," he bellowed, "that blackbird will be tied to the end of my bed, and I will watch him carefully and find out the secret of his magic!"

13

So that night the blackbird was tied to the king's bedpost, and the king lay awake, listening. In the middle of the night the king heard the blackbird calling to the river. Straight away the river came flowing out of the blackbird's ear. It covered the floor, it poured under the door, it flowed through the palace.

The king's bed began to float, his blankets were wet, his pajamas clung to his skin. Soon he was quivering and quaking, shivering and shaking with the cold.

"Very w-well, Mr. B-Blackbird," he trembled, "I give in. Take your wife and g-go away." The king reached up above his bed and opened the door of the silver cage, and he reached to the foot of the bed and cut the knots from the bedpost.

The blackbird and his wife flew out of the window, over the rooftops, over the fields and the forests until they came to their tree. And as the bright sun rose into the sky, they sang together, and if you'd been listening it would have been as though gold and silver rain had fallen into your ears.

The Two Little Elves
◇ CHILEAN ◇

A story, a story! Let it go, let it come! Once upon a time there were two brothers, one was rich and the other was poor.

The rich brother had horses and cows and sheep, he had geese and ducks and chickens, he had houses and barns and open fields.

The poor brother had four old donkeys and a little tumbledown hut for a home. And did the rich brother help the poor brother? No, he did not.

He didn't speak to him. He wouldn't even look at him when they passed on the road.

Every day the poor brother would take his four donkeys into the forest. Every day he would cut sticks and load them onto the donkeys' backs. And every day he would take the sticks to market and sell them for a few copper coins — just enough money to buy some moldy vegetables for thin soup and some torn rags for thin clothes for his wife and children.

One day, while the poor brother was busy chopping wood and loading sticks, he heard the sound of singing:

MONDAY AND TUESDAY, WEDNESDAY THREE.
MONDAY AND TUESDAY, WEDNESDAY THREE.

He turned and saw that two little elves had appeared out of the shadows between the trees. They were singing and as they sang they danced from foot to foot:

MONDAY AND TUESDAY, WEDNESDAY THREE.
MONDAY AND TUESDAY, WEDNESDAY THREE.

Well, the poor brother knew that song as well, and so he joined in:

THURSDAY AND FRIDAY, SATURDAY SIX.
THURSDAY AND FRIDAY, SATURDAY SIX.

The two elves stopped dancing, they looked at one another and laughed:

"What a beautiful verse!"

They ran across to the poor brother:

"Sing it again! Sing it again!"

The poor brother shook his head:

"Haven't you heard it before?"

"No!"

So the poor brother sang again:

THURSDAY AND FRIDAY, SATURDAY SIX.
THURSDAY AND FRIDAY, SATURDAY SIX.

The two little elves danced and laughed.

"It's the song of the days," said the poor brother, "it's the song of all the days, put it together and it goes like this my little friends":

MONDAY AND TUESDAY, WEDNESDAY THREE.
THURSDAY AND FRIDAY, SATURDAY SIX.

He taught them the song and they were delighted with it. Soon they were dancing and singing with all their hearts:

MONDAY AND TUESDAY, WEDNESDAY THREE.
THURSDAY AND FRIDAY, SATURDAY SIX.

Then they stopped and looked at one another again.

"Shouldn't we give him something, shouldn't we give him something for his song?"

They nodded at each other and laughed.

"We'll each give him a foot."

Then each of the elves took a little knife from his pocket and cut off his foot. They hopped across to the poor brother.

"No more chopping sticks for you. These are wishing feet. Wish for whatever you want, a breathful of wishes for each foot — then the foot will vanish."

And the two little elves hopped away between the trees singing:

MONDAY AND TUESDAY, WEDNESDAY THREE.
THURSDAY AND FRIDAY, SATURDAY SIX.

Well, the poor brother went home to his little tumbledown hut. His wife was standing in the doorway, and his three hungry children were tugging at her raggedy skirts. When they saw him coming through the trees they started shouting: "What's for supper, Daddy? What's for supper?"

He looked at them and grinned: "A better supper than you've ever dreamt of, my darlings."

He reached into his pocket and took out a tiny foot. He held it in the palm of his hand, took a deep breath and began to wish:

"Little foot, little foot, I wish for the finest food for all my family, for chickens and geese in the yard, for sheep, cows, horses in the barns, and for fields beyond as far as the eye can see."

No sooner were the words spoken than the foot vanished and everything he had wished for was there before him. He and his wife and the three children sat down at the splintery table in the tumbledown hut and ate the most wonderful food they had ever tasted. And as they ate, they listened to the clucking of chickens, the hissing of geese, the bleating of sheep, the mooing of cows and the whinnying of horses. And when they could eat no more, the poor brother reached into his other pocket and took out the other foot.

"Little foot, little foot, I wish for the finest clothes on our backs, for palaces with golden roofs filled from floor to ceiling with money, with silver beds and golden tables and floors studded with diamonds."

Straight away his wish was granted and the second foot was gone.

Well, the weeks passed and the months passed and the poor man (who was poor no longer) and his family were happy.

Then one day, the rich and greedy brother came to pay a visit. Soon enough, he was sitting at a golden table nibbling the finest food.

"My brother," he said, "how have you had such luck? You're living like a king these days, and not so long ago you were selling sticks in the marketplace. What happened?"

The poor brother smiled. "I was out in the forest and I met two little elves. I taught them a new verse to their song and they gave me two wishes in return."

"Aha," thought the rich and greedy brother, "two can play at that game!"

The next day, he dressed himself in raggedy clothes, he took four donkeys and he made his way into the forest. He began cutting sticks with his axe. He hadn't been cutting for long when he heard the sound of voices:

MONDAY AND TUESDAY, WEDNESDAY THREE.
THURSDAY AND FRIDAY, SATURDAY SIX.

He turned and saw the little elves. They had two feet apiece and they were singing and dancing:

MONDAY AND TUESDAY, WEDNESDAY THREE.
THURSDAY AND FRIDAY, SATURDAY SIX.

The rich brother took a deep breath and shouted:

SUNDAY MAKES SEVEN!

The two elves stopped dancing, they looked at one another and laughed:
"What a beautiful verse! Sing it again, sing it again."

The rich brother shouted:

SUNDAY MAKES SEVEN!
SUNDAY MAKES SEVEN!

"Now, give me two wishes; can't you see what a poor woodcutter I am?'

The elves looked at each other and nodded. Each of them took a little knife and cut off his foot. They gave the two feet to the rich brother.

"A breathful of wishes for each foot," they said, "and then it disappears."

And they hopped away singing:

MONDAY AND TUESDAY, WEDNESDAY THREE.
THURSDAY AND FRIDAY, SATURDAY SIX,
SUNDAY MAKES SEVEN.

Well, the rich brother hurried home to his wife. She was standing in the doorway of their fine farmhouse holding their plump little baby daughter in her arms.

"Look what I've got!" he shouted, and he pulled one of the tiny feet out of his pocket. "This is a wishing foot."

His wife looked at him and shook her head. "A wishing foot," she said, "what nonsense you talk."

She reached across and snatched the tiny foot out of his hand. "We'll soon see if this is a wishing foot!"

Before the rich brother could stop her she said, "Wishing foot, if wishing foot you be, put whiskers and beard onto my baby's cheeks and chin."

No sooner were the words spoken than the foot vanished and the baby's face was covered with a thick black bristling beard. The wife screamed. She ran and fetched a pair of scissors, but the more she snipped away the black beard, the thicker it grew back.

The baby was bawling, his wife was shrieking, and the rich brother knew there was only one thing to be done.

He pulled the other foot from his pocket:

"Little foot, take away my baby's beard."

Straight away the beard was gone and the foot had vanished.

He looked at his wife, and his wife looked at him.

"Now both our wishes are fled, and there are no more to be had —
because seven is as many days as a week holds."

And that's the end of my story...but I'll tell you a secret. I've been told
that those two elves have found the beginning of a new song:

JANUARY AND FEBRUARY, MARCH THREE.
JANUARY AND FEBRUARY, MARCH THREE.

Keep your eyes and your ears open. You might meet them, you might be
able to teach them some more, you might be given two wishing feet...

The Mightiest Mouse that ever Nibbled Fat

INUIT

Once upon a time there lived a little gray mouse. More than anything else in the world he wanted to be famous — so famous that people would still be talking about him in a thousand years. Sometimes in the middle of the night he would climb up onto the roof of the hut where he lived, and he would lift up his little pink paws until it seemed that the moon was caught between them.

"Look at me," he would shout. "I can hold the moon. I am the mightiest mouse that ever nibbled fat!"

One morning, the little mouse woke up in his nest under the shelf in a corner of the hut, and he saw that a terrible fire was blazing in the doorway of the hut. There was yellow light pouring in, and it was growing brighter with every moment that passed. The little mouse leapt to his feet and flicked his tail from side to side.

"If I ran through those flames and fetched water," he thought to himself, "then the world would know what a brave mouse I am."

He closed his eyes and he ran. He ran into the fire. He ran through the flames and out of the door. And it wasn't hot!

His fur wasn't burnt at all. He began to shout, "I'm the mightiest mouse that ever nibbled fat!" Then he opened his eyes and looked over his shoulder. The terrible fire was nothing but the sunlight shining through the doorway. It was nothing but yellow sunshine.

"Oh dear, perhaps the world is harder to please than I thought."

Then he saw that in front of him there was a hill. A great yellow hill stretching high above his head.

"If I jumped up onto that hill in one bound," he thought to himself, "then the world would know what a powerful mouse I am."

He closed his eyes and he jumped. He jumped with all his strength and he landed fair and square on the top of the hill. It wasn't far! His feet didn't hurt at all. He began to shout, "I'm the mightiest mouse that ever nibbled fat!" Then he opened his eyes and looked over his shoulder. The great hill was nothing but a little heap of sand. It was nothing but a panful of yellow sand.

"Oh dear, perhaps the world is harder to please than I thought."

Then he saw that in front of him there was a lake. A lake so wide that he could hardly see across to the other side. "If I paddle over that lake," he thought to himself, "then the world would know what a fearless mouse I am."

He jumped onto a leaf and, using a blade of grass for an oar, paddled across the wide lake. It didn't seem to take very long. When he reached the other side, he was tired, so he laid down to sleep, thinking, "I'm the mightiest mouse that ever nibbled fat!"

When he woke up again, he opened his eyes and looked over his shoulder. The wide lake was nothing but a man's footprint, full of muddy water.

"Oh dear, perhaps the world is harder to please than I thought."

He traveled on for a while until he saw something tall and thin. It looked like a great pole stretching up into the sky. "Aha," the mouse thought to himself. "That must be the pole that holds up the sky. If I were to cut it down, then the whole sky would come crashing down and the world would surely remember me for that!"

He closed his eyes and he began to nibble and gnaw at the foot of the pole. He nibbled and gnawed until it toppled and fell. It didn't take long.

"I'm the mightiest mouse that ever nibbled fat!"

He put his paws over his ears and waited for the sky to come down, but nothing happened. He opened one eye and then the other. He looked up and the sky was as blue and high as it had always been. He looked over his shoulder and the great pole was nothing but a tall blade of grass lying on the ground.

"Oh dear, perhaps the world is harder to please than I thought."

And he continued his journey.

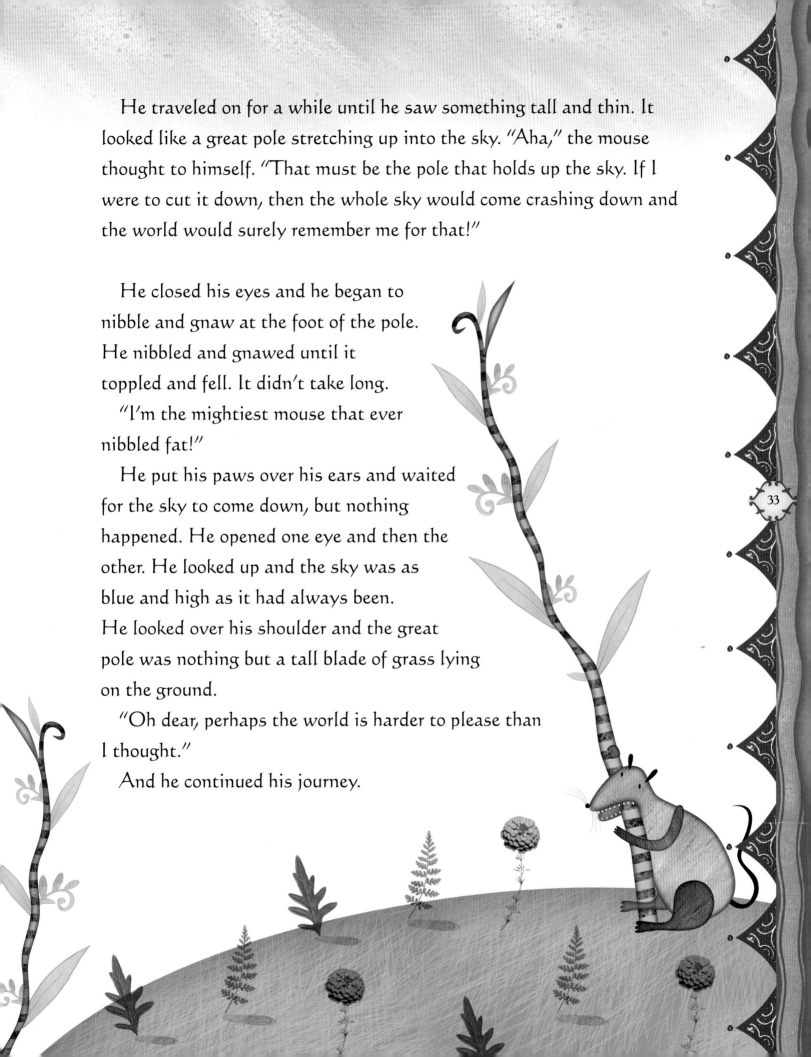

Then he saw a mountain — a gray mountain with snowy crags reaching high into the clouds. "If I were to move that mountain," he thought to himself, "then surely the world would never forget me."

It took him many days, traveling over the tundra, to reach that mountain. It took him many weeks to dig around it with his claws.

It took him many years to carry the mountain
grain by grain, pebble by pebble, stone by stone, from
there to here. It took him many, many, many years to shift
that whole mountain to where it is now. And when it was
all finished, the little mouse rubbed his eyes and looked over
his shoulder.

Yes — it was a mountain! And the people called it Mouse
Mountain, and they gathered around him and said, "You are the
mightiest mouse that ever nibbled fat!"

That was a thousand years ago — and they're talking about him
still. And so am I!

Winter and Summer
SENECA

◇ Once upon a time, the world was covered with snow. The fields and the forests, the lakes and the mountains, were white with snow. And high on a hill stood Winter, watching over the wide, white world with eyes as sharp as icicles. But even Winter felt cold; his bones were made of ice, his skin was made of snow, he was cold from head to toe. He was stiff and aching with cold, and he longed for just a little warmth. He dreamt of glowing fires and warm clothes.

One day he decided to try and find the warmth he had dreamt about. He strode down the hill, the icy wind whistling between his teeth.

He saw two children sliding on the ice. One of them was wearing a pair of fur mittens over her hands, and one was wearing a fur hood over his head. Winter stopped and stared at them, then he spoke:

> "I'm frozen through and through and through,
> Bones of ice and skin of snow,
> I'm colder than you, than you, than you,
> Bones of ice and skin of snow,
> Give me your mittens and your hood of fur NOW!"

And he blew up a blizzard with his breath. The two children were so frightened that they took off their mittens and hood and gave them to Winter. And Winter snatched them out of the children's hands. He stretched the mittens over his great white fists, he stretched the hood over his great white head, and he set off striding through the forest.

Then he saw a hunter following tracks across the snow. The hunter was wearing a thick fur cloak over his shoulders. Winter stopped and stared at him, and then he spoke:

"I'm frozen through and through and through,
Bones of ice and skin of snow,
I'm colder than you, than you, than you,
Bones of ice and skin of snow,
Give me your cloak of fur NOW!"

And he blew up a blizzard with his breath. The hunter was so frightened that he took off his cloak and gave it to Winter. And Winter snatched it out of the hunter's hands, stretched it over his great, white shoulders, and set off striding through the forest.

Then he saw a hut at the edge of the forest, and standing in the doorway was an old woman. She was wearing a pair of thick fur boots on her feet. Winter stopped and stared at her, and then he spoke:

"I'm frozen through and through and through,
Bones of ice and skin of snow,
I'm colder than you, than you, than you,
Bones of ice and skin of snow,
Give me your boots of fur NOW!"

And he blew up a blizzard with his breath. But the old woman,
whose name was Summer, was not the least tiny bit frightened of Winter.

"Of course you can have my boots," she said. "Of course you can.
But I'm not taking them off here, out in the bitter cold. If you want
my boots then you must come inside and wait while I take them off in
the warmth."

"Very well," said Winter, and he followed the old woman into the
hut. Inside there was a beautiful, blazing fire.

"Sit down here and warm yourself in the firelight while I take my
boots off."

So Winter sat down and stretched his feet and hands toward the fire.

This was the warmth he had been dreaming about.

Old Summer left him sitting there for a while, then she said:

"Do you feel any warmer now?"

"No! I'm frozen through and through. I'm so cold I can't feel my hands, I can't feel my feet, my shoulders are as cold as a snowdrift."

"Well," said old Summer. "That won't do."

And she threw some more wood onto the fire.

"Do you feel any warmer now?"

"No! I'm frozen through and through. I'm so cold I can't feel my arms, I can't feel my legs, my neck is as cold as an iceberg."

"Oh dear, oh dear," said old Summer, and she threw some more wood onto the fire. "Do you feel any warmer now?"

But all that was left of Winter was a lump of snow the size of a snowball, and on the floor in front of the fire was a big puddle of slushy sloshy water. And from the lump of snow came a thin voice: "I'm still cold…"

And then Winter was gone, and old Summer rubbed her hands together and laughed. She ran across and threw open the door of her hut. Outside, the sun was shining, the fields were brown, the forests were green, the lakes were blue and the gray mountains had just a little snow shimmering on their tops. Winter was gone!

The old woman called to the children and gave them back their hood and mittens. She called to the hunter and gave him back his warm cloak. And they thanked old Summer…but they wouldn't be needing the fur anymore, not for a while anyway!

43

The Strange Visitor
SCOTTISH

Once upon a time, in a dark wood there was a dark house. And
in that dark house there was a dark door. And beyond that dark
door there was a dark and shadowy room with a rocking chair
and one candle burning. And sitting in the rocking chair was
an old woman, wrinkled as an old winter's apple, bent
over the sewing that lay on her lap.

And still she sat, and still she sewed, and still she wished for company.

And as she wished, the door burst open and in came two big, big feet. They walked across the room and stood in front of her rocking chair.

And still she sat, and still she sewed, and still she wished for company.

And in through the door came two thin, thin, knock-kneed legs, and they floated across the room and stood on the big, big feet.

And still she sat, and still she sewed, and still she wished for company.

45

And in through the door came a pair of wide, wide hips, and they floated across the room and sat on the thin, thin legs.

And still she sat, and still she sewed, and still she wished for company.

And in through the door came a wee, wee waist and it floated across the room and landed on the wide, wide hips.

And still she sat, and still she sewed, and still she wished for company.

And in through the door came a pair of broad, broad shoulders, and they floated across the room and eased themselves down onto the wee, wee waist.

And still she sat, and still she sewed, and still she wished for company.

And in through the door came two thin, thin, dingling, dangling arms, and they floated across the room and hung themselves from the broad, broad shoulders.

And still she sat, and still she sewed, and still she wished for company.

And in through the door came two strong, strong hands, and they floated across the room and fitted themselves to the ends of the thin, thin arms.

And still she sat, and still she sewed, and still she wished for company.

And in through the door came a narrow, narrow neck, and it floated across the room and perched between the broad, broad shoulders.

And still she sat, and still she sewed, and still she wished for company.

And last of all, in through the door came a huge, huge head, blinking its eyes and clacking its teeth, and it floated across the room and dropped down onto the narrow, narrow neck.

And still she sat, and still she sewed...but then she looked at the strange visitor and suddenly she saw that she had got some company at last.

"Tell me," she said, "why have you got such big, big feet?"

"MUCH TRAMPING, MUCH TRAMPING!"

"And why have you got such thin, thin legs?"

"TOO MUCH WATER, TOO LITTLE MEAT!"

"And why have you got such wide, wide hips?"

"MUCH SITTING, MUCH SITTING!"

"And why have you got such a wee, wee waist?"

"TOO MUCH WATER, TOO LITTLE MEAT!"

"And why have you got such broad, broad shoulders?"

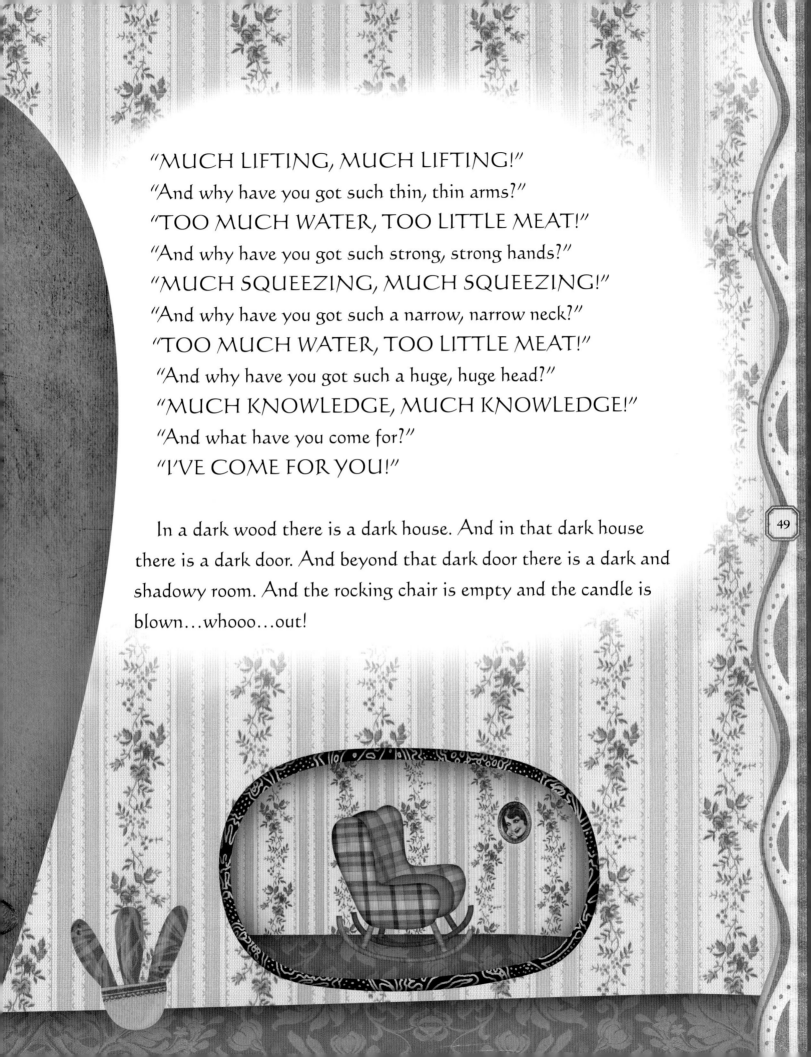

"MUCH LIFTING, MUCH LIFTING!"

"And why have you got such thin, thin arms?"

"TOO MUCH WATER, TOO LITTLE MEAT!"

"And why have you got such strong, strong hands?"

"MUCH SQUEEZING, MUCH SQUEEZING!"

"And why have you got such a narrow, narrow neck?"

"TOO MUCH WATER, TOO LITTLE MEAT!"

"And why have you got such a huge, huge head?"

"MUCH KNOWLEDGE, MUCH KNOWLEDGE!"

"And what have you come for?"

"I'VE COME FOR YOU!"

In a dark wood there is a dark house. And in that dark house there is a dark door. And beyond that dark door there is a dark and shadowy room. And the rocking chair is empty and the candle is blown…whooo…out!

Who Lives in the Skull?

Once upon a time, on the top of a hill, there was a horse's skull. It had been lying there for a long time and it was as clean and white as marble and as hollow as a seashell. One day a mouse saw the skull and thought to himself, "That would be a fine place to live." So he knocked on the white bone of the skull and said, "Hello! I'm Mr. Twitchery Snitchery Nibble by Night! Does anyone live inside this skull?"

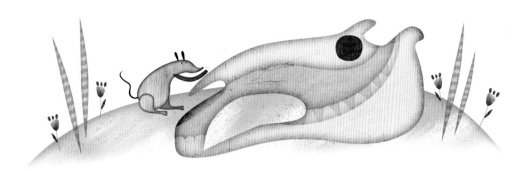

There was no answer, so the mouse crawled inside and set up house — and very snug it was. Then one day a frog came knocking on the white bone. "Hello! I'm Mr. Hoppity Ploppity Paddle the Pond! Does anyone live inside this skull?"

"Only me, Mr. Twitchery Snitchery Nibble by Night. Come inside, there's room enough for two."

So the frog crawled inside and they set up house together — and very snug it was.

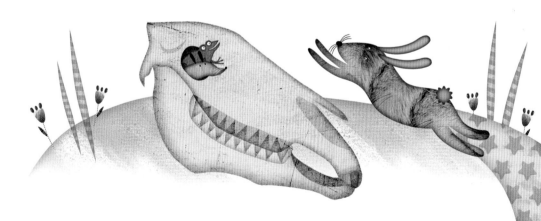

And then one day a hare came knocking on the white bone. "Hello! I'm Mr. Lollopy Gallopy King of the Corn! Does anyone live inside this skull?"

"Only us, Mr. Twitchery Snitchery Nibble by Night and Mr. Hoppity Ploppity Paddle the Pond. Come inside, there's room enough for three." So the hare crawled inside and they set up house together — and very snug it was, if a little cramped.

Then one day a fox came knocking on the white bone. "Hello! I'm Mr. Knavery Knifery Thief of the Coop! Does anyone live inside this skull?"

"Only us, Mr. Twitchery Snitchery Nibble by Night, Mr. Hoppity Ploppity Paddle the Pond and Mr. Lollopy Gallopy King of the Corn. Come inside, there's room enough for four." So the fox crawled inside and they set up house together — and very snug it was, if a little squashed.

Then one day a wolf came knocking on the white bone. "Hello! I'm Mr. Slavering Slobbering Tongue on the Tilt! Does anyone live inside this skull?"

"Only us, Mr. Twitchery Snitchery Nibble by Night, Mr. Hoppity Ploppity Paddle the Pond, Mr. Lollopy Gallopy King of the Corn and Mr. Knavery Knifery Thief of the Coop. Come inside, there's room enough for five." So the wolf crawled inside and they set up house together — and very snug it was, but very squashed.

And then one day a bear came knocking on the white bone. "Hello! I'm Mr. Lumbersome Cumbersome Sit on the Lot! Does anyone live inside this skull?"

And Mr. Twitchery Snitchery Nibble by Night,

Mr. Hoppity Ploppity Paddle the Pond,

Mr. Lollopy Gallopy King of the Corn,

Mr. Knavery Knifery Thief of the Coop and

Mr. Slavering Slobbering Tongue on the Tilt,

squashed together in the skull and knowing there wasn't room enough for six, all shouted at once, "No! Nobody lives here! Nobody lives here at all!"

And Mr. Lumbersome Cumbersome Sit on the Lot said, "Well, that's all right then…" And he sat down on top of the skull. He sat down on top of the lot of them.

CRUNCH.

And whether any of them got out in time or whether they didn't, I don't know. But one thing I do know is this: that bear is still pulling splinters of white bone out of his backside to this very day.

When you tell this story you can make one hand the skull, and the fingers and thumb of the other hand the animals that go inside. Choose one of your listeners to be the bear who sits on them all!

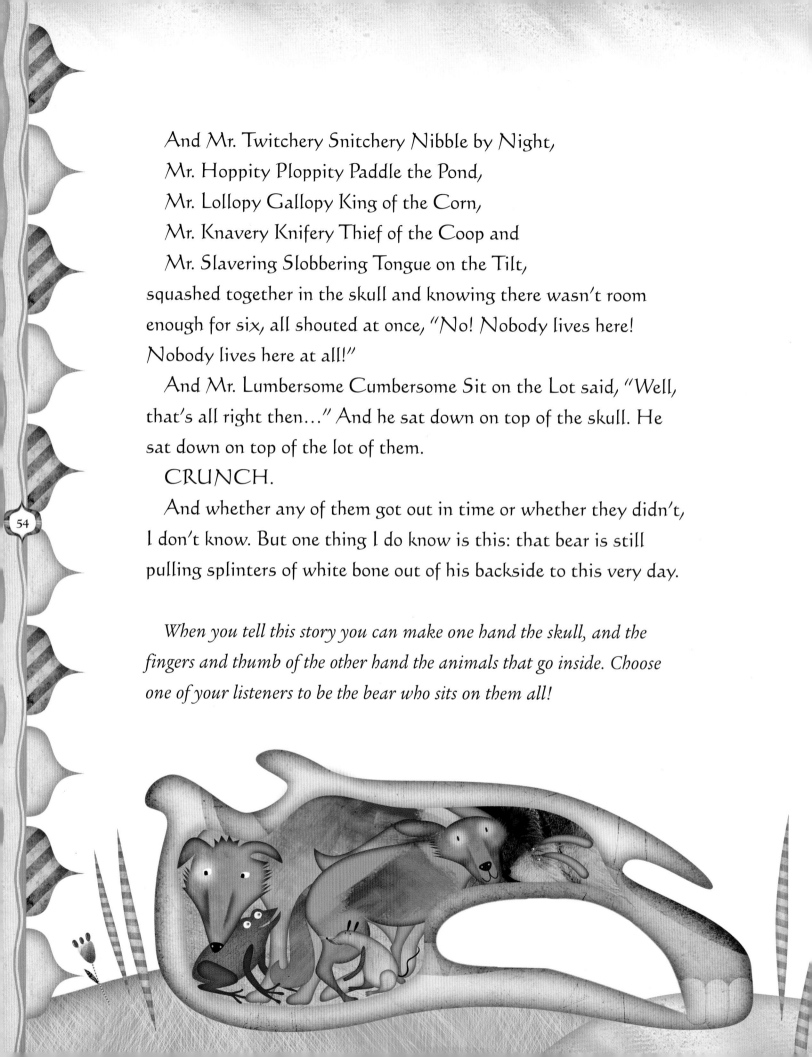

The Hunter's Five Sons
◇ WEST AFRICAN ◇

Once upon a time there lived a hunter and his wife and their four fine sons. The hunter's wife was expecting her fifth baby; sometimes she could feel it kicking against her insides.

"It'll be another boy," she would say. "Another fine strong boy, just like his brothers."

One day the hunter went out into the forest with his spear and his bow and his quiver full of arrows, and at the end of the day he didn't come home. His wife and his four sons stayed up all night waiting for him, but still he didn't come home. And his wife and his four sons wept for him.

Two weeks passed and he didn't come home. And his wife and his four sons dried their tears.

A month passed and he didn't come home. And his wife and four sons forgot about him. They forgot all about the hunter with his spear and his bow and his quiver full of arrows.

Two months passed and the new baby was born, and he was a fine strong boy just like his brothers. The baby grew. Soon he was crawling and soon he was walking and then he began to talk. And the very first words he said were, "Where's my Daddy?"

That youngest one looked at his mother and his four fine brothers and he said, "Where's my Daddy?"

And they put their hands to their heads. "We had forgotten about him! We had forgotten all about him! He went into the forest and he never came home."

And their mother said, "My sons, you must go and look for him." The four brothers said, "Yes, our mother is right. We must go into the forest and look for him."

They set off together. First they found a spear lying on the ground, then they found a bow and a quiver full of arrows, and then they found the hunter's white bones scattered across the forest floor.

The first brother said, "It's a lucky thing that I have the power to bring the bones together!" And he blew on the scattered bones and they jumped and rattled and locked together into the shape of a skeleton.

The second brother said, "It's a lucky thing that I have the power to put flesh and skin onto the bones!" And he blew onto the skeleton, and flesh and skin came and covered the bones, and there was the hunter lying on the ground.

The third brother said, "It's a lucky thing that I have the power to put life into the body!" And he blew, and the hunter's heart began to beat and his body to breathe, as though he was sleeping.

The fourth brother said, "It's a lucky thing that I have the power to put movement into the body!"

And he breathed on the hunter, and the hunter sat up and looked about himself.

"Where have I been?" he asked.

And his sons answered, "Once you were dead, but now you're alive!"

And the hunter nodded and smiled at his sons, and he picked up his spear and his bow and his quiver full of arrows and he made his way home. His sons followed him. His wife was happy to see him; she threw her arms around his neck and kissed him. "You had been away for so long that we had forgotten you," she said.

The hunter nodded and smiled at his wife and he sat down by the fire.

He picked up a knife and a lump of hard black ebony wood and he began to carve. He carved quietly and his sons sat and watched him. He carved all night. He carved for a week. He carved for a month.

It was beautiful — it was the most beautiful carving they had seen in their lives. All the animals and birds of the forest were in it, all the trees and the flowers. For two months he carved, and then he rubbed oil into the wood and polished it with a piece of cloth.

He looked at his family. "This is for the one that saved my life," he said.

And his wife said, "Then it is mine. I sent them out into the forest to search for you."

And the first brother said, "No, it is mine. I brought all your bones together."

And the second brother said, "No, it is mine. I put flesh and skin onto your bones."

And the third brother said, "No, it is mine. I gave you life."

And the fourth brother said, "No, it is mine. I gave you movement."

The hunter looked at them all, and smiled and shook his head.

"No," he said, "it is for the little one, my youngest son. He was the one who remembered me, and as long as a person is remembered by someone, he is not altogether dead." And he lifted the fifth son onto his knee and kissed his head and pressed the beautiful carving of hard black ebony wood into his little hands.

Sources for the Stories

The Blackbird and his Wife

I've come across several versions of this Indian story. It follows a universal theme – the hero and his helpers – but with the zaniness that I've always enjoyed. A good introduction to the wealth of Indian stories is J.E.B. Gray's **Indian Tales and Legends** (Oxford University Press, 1961).

The Two Little Elves

There are versions of this story all over Europe, so I imagine this Chilean variation came originally from Spain. I found it in Yolando Pino-Saavedra's **Folktales of Chile** (R & K Paul, 1968).

The Mightiest Mouse that ever Nibbled Fat

I came across this Inuit tale in an old anthology (long out of print) entitled **Folk Tales of all Nations**, edited by F.H. Lee (Harrap, 1931). A goldmine if you can find it!

Winter and Summer

When I was staying in New York State in the mid-seventies, I found the germ of this story in an old (nineteenth century, I think) collection of Seneca myths. I've been telling it ever since.

The Strange Visitor

Another one I've been telling for years! It's one of those tales that seems inconsequential on the page, but has a life of its own when it's spoken aloud. For more Scottish tales, read any of Duncan Williamson's books (published by Canongate, Edinburgh), or Neil Philip's **Penguin Book of Scottish Folk Tales** (Penguin, Harmondsworth, 1995).

Who Lives in the Skull?

When I was a boy, I used to visit Arthur Ransome and his Russian wife in the Lake District – he was my great uncle. This story comes from his collection of Russian folktales, **Old Peter's Russian Tales** (Nelson, London, 1971).

The Hunter's Five Sons

This simple, profound story was first told to me by Jan Blake – a magnificent Jamaican-African storyteller. The story's original title is **The Cow-Tail Switch**.

Barefoot Books
Celebrating Art and Story

At Barefoot Books, we celebrate art and story that opens
the hearts and minds of children from all walks of life, inspiring
them to read deeper, search further, and explore their own creative gifts.
Taking our inspiration from many different cultures, we focus on themes that
encourage independence of spirit, enthusiasm for learning, and sharing of
the world's diversity. Interactive, playful and beautiful, our products
combine the best of the present with the best of the past to
educate our children as the caretakers of tomorrow.

Live Barefoot!
Join us at **www.barefootbooks.com**